Josie's Big Jump   JNEE

£2.50

L 5/9

The Waterhole

Archie's House

The Plane

The Homestead

Mitzi's

Ned's Caravan

The Windmill

JN 03892457

Copyright © Spellbound Entertainment Limited and Famous Flying Films Limited 2004

Published by Ladybird Books Ltd

A Penguin Company

80 Strand, London WC2R 0RL

Penguin Books Australia Ltd., Camberwell, Victoria, Australia

Penguin Books (NZ) Ltd., Private Bag 102902, NSMC, Auckland, New Zealand

www.ladybird.co.uk

3 5 7 9 10 8 6 4 2

Josie's
Big Jump

Ladybird

One sleepy day, deep in the Australian outback, Josie the little kangaroo decided she wanted to learn how to skip.

Josie worked in the general store, where there were lots of skipping ropes for sale. Shyly, Josie chose one. Then, she stepped over the rope, took a deep breath, whipped the rope over her head and jumped!

BOING! Josie jumped up into the air, but as the rope came down it caught in her big feet! Skipping was harder than it looked.

Just then, there was a *flip-flop-skippety* sort of noise. In came Mitzi, with *her* skipping rope. Mitzi was a brilliant skipper, even in flip-flops.

"Hi Josie!" called Mitzi, skilfully skipping. "Will you skip to the waterhole with me? It'll be fun!"

"I'm busy," Josie said, shyly. She didn't want Mitzi to know how bad she was at skipping. "Maybe later."

"If I come back later," said Mitzi, "will you *promise* to come skipping with me? *PROMISE*?"

"Okay. I . . . I promise," sighed Josie. Mitzi skipped off happily, but Josie was worried. Soon Mitzi would know she couldn't skip at all!

Josie needed some help.

Meanwhile, at the Koala Brothers'
homestead, it was washing day.
Frank and Buster were running a
little late, and would need some
help from Ned.

"Ned, would you mind hanging out
our washing for us?" asked Frank.
"We have to go out on patrol in
the plane."

Ned knew that Frank and Buster wouldn't ask him for help if it wasn't important. "Okay," he agreed, kindly.

"Thanks, Ned!" chorused the Koala Brothers, as they rushed to the plane.

Once they'd taken off, Ned looked at the washing. There was an awful lot. How would it all fit on the line?

Frank and Buster needed to put petrol in their plane, so they flew to the pump at the general store. They both thought Josie seemed very sad.

"What's wrong, Josie?" asked Frank.

"I can't skip!" sighed Josie. "And I *really* want to!"

"Why?" asked Buster in surprise. Josie was close to tears.

"Because I promised Mitzi I'd go skipping with her this afternoon!"

Frank and Buster nodded. "Don't worry. We'll think of something."

"Really?" sniffed Josie.

"Sure!" Frank beamed at her. "We're here to help!"

Josie was sure the Koala Brothers
would find a way to help her. But
in the meantime, she went into the
outback to practise some more.

She tried and tried. She jumped
about and pranced about – she even
danced about – but each time she

bounced high up in the air, she would always tangle up her feet in the skipping rope on the way back down.

After a while, George the turtle postman came by. "Oh, dear!" he cried. "You tripped! Keep practising, Josie. Practice makes perfect!"

Josie tried again – and got her toes in a total tangle as usual. "Practice doesn't make perfect," she sighed. "Practice makes *knots*!"

It wasn't long before Alice came by on her scooter. "Josie!" she cried. "What are you doing out here in the middle of nowhere?"

"I'm learning to skip," poor Josie said, sadly. "Can you skip, Alice? Show me how you do it!"

Alice agreed, and was soon skipping all about the place. "A hop, skip and a jump always works for me!" she explained.

Josie had a go – and fell over her feet for the two-hundredth time. "It doesn't work for *me*," she muttered, miserably. "Oh, I do hope Frank and Buster can think of a way to help me . . ."

Meanwhile, back at the homestead, Frank and Buster were trying to help Ned with the washing! But the clothesline just wasn't long enough.

"We've got a problem, Buster," said Frank.

All of a sudden, Buster came up with a brilliant idea. "I've got it!" he cried. "We need two ropes joined together!"

"*Two* ropes?" Frank and Ned gasped at the same time.

"Yes!" Buster carried on. "To make a longer washing line!"

So Frank, Buster and Ned set to work. They took two ropes and tied them together. Then they wrapped each end of the rope round the top of a tall pole. The new, improved, two-rope washing line had room for all the washing to hang out to dry!

"Wow, Buster!" chirped Ned in wonder. "You're brilliant!"

Frank was about to agree when he remembered something. "Buster! We said we'd help Josie to learn to skip."

They'd forgotten all about Josie!

The Koala Brothers thought hard about how they could help their good friend. They needed a sure-fire skipping scheme . . . and fast.

"Maybe she could go to skipping classes?" suggested Buster.

"There's no time," Frank pointed out. If only they hadn't spent the *whole* morning wrestling with all that wet washing!

Frank looked up at the extra-long clothesline – and suddenly, he had a brilliant brainwave!

"Buster," Frank said slowly, a broad smile spreading over his face. "Have we got any more lengths of rope? I've got an idea . . ."

Back at the store, Josie had given up all hope of learning to skip when she saw the Koala Brothers walking towards her.

"How're you getting on, Josie?" asked Frank, kindly.

Josie was very close to tears. "I've tried and tried but I *still* can't skip!" she wailed.

Then Frank pulled something from behind his back. It was two ropes, tied together. "If you've got big jumping feet, Josie, you need a long rope," he explained. "Long enough for it to go right over your head!"

Buster nodded in agreement. "Go on, Josie," he said. "Try it!"

So, Josie *did* try it. She stepped over the extra-long rope, took a deep breath, whipped the rope over her head and jumped!

BOING! Josie jumped high up into the air just as she always did, but *this* time, the rope went *under* her feet and *over* her head, with not *one single toe* tangling up in the rope! BOING! She did it again, and then again!

"Look! I CAN SKIP!" she squealed, jumping as high as could be. "Thanks, Frank! Thanks, Buster!"

Just then, Mitzi came skipping along.

"Hi, Josie!" Mitzi called. "You promised you'd come skipping with me. Are you ready?"

"Yeah!" beamed Josie. "Catch me if you can!"

"Wow!" gasped Mitzi as Josie jumped joyfully about, as skilled a skipper as you ever did see. "I've never seen anybody skip as fast as you, Josie. You're the *best*!"

Frank and Buster smiled at each other. Josie *had* learned to skip after all. In fact, she'd become the fastest skipper in the outback – with a little help from the Koala Brothers!

The General Store

Alice's House

Post Office

The Post B